THE BUBONIC BUILDERS

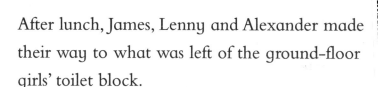

After lunch, James, Lenny and Alexander made their way to what was left of the ground-floor girls' toilet block.

'There's only one builder in there again – the same bloke I spoke to last time,' James whispered.

'I think he's talking to himself,' Alexander hissed.

James walked forwards carefully, standing to the side to avoid the builder's swinging hammer. 'Excuse me! Excuse me, sir . . .'

The man didn't look round. James tried again.

'Hi, it's me – I was in here before . . .'

With one extra-wild swing, the builder smashed the heavy hammer hard down on to his hand.

The boys stared on in horror. The builder carried on hammering, not noticing that one of his fingers had been completely smashed off. Green goo dripped on to the plaster dust below.

St Sebastian's School in Grimesford is the pits. No, really – it is.

Every year, the high school sinks a bit further into the boggy plague pit beneath it and, every year, the ghosts of the plague victims buried underneath it become a bit more cranky.

Egged on by their spooky ringleader, Edith Codd, they decide to get their own back – and they're willing to play dirty. *Really* dirty.

They kick up a stink by causing as much mischief as in inhumanly possible so as to get St Sebastian's closed down once and for all.

But what they haven't reckoned on is year-seven new boy, James Simpson and his friends Alexander and Lenny.

The question is, are the gang up to the challenge of laying St Sebastian's paranormal problem to rest, or will their school remain forever frightful?

There's only one way to find out . . .

www.too-ghoul.com

TOO GHOUL FOR SCHOOL

THE BUBONIC BUILDERS

B. STRANGE

EGMONT

Special thanks to:

Lynn Huggins-Cooper, St John's Walworth Church of England Primary School and Belmont Primary School

EGMONT
We bring stories to life

Published in Great Britain 2007
by Egmont UK Limited
239 Kensington High Street, London W8 6SA

Text & illustrations © 2007 Egmont UK Ltd
Text by Lynn Huggins-Cooper
Illustrations by Pulsar Studio (Beehive Illustration)

ISBN 978 1 4052 3234 0

3 5 7 9 10 8 6 4

A CIP catalogue record for this title is available
from the British Library

Typeset by Avon DataSet Ltd, Bidford on Avon, Warwickshire
Printed and bound in Great Britain by the CPI Group

'More books – I love it!'
Ashley, age 11

'It's disgusting. . .'
Joe, age 10

'. . . it's all good!'
Alexander, age 9

'. . . loads of excitement and really gross!'
Jay, age 9

'I like the way there's the brainy boy,
the brawny boy and the cool boy that form a
team of friends'
Charlie, age 10

'That ghost Edith is wicked'
Matthew, age 11

'This is really good and funny!'
Sam, age 9

School versus...

Year-seven new boy
and chief spook-hunter

James Simpson

Headmaster's son
and official brainiac

Alexander Tick

Strong as an ox,
gentle as an
unusually tall lamb

Lenny Maxwell

...Ghoul!

Loud-mouthed ringleader of the plague-pit ghosts

Edith Codd

Young ghost and a secret wannabe St Sebastian's pupil

William Scroggins

Bone idle ex-leech merchant with a taste for all things gross

Ambrose Harbottle

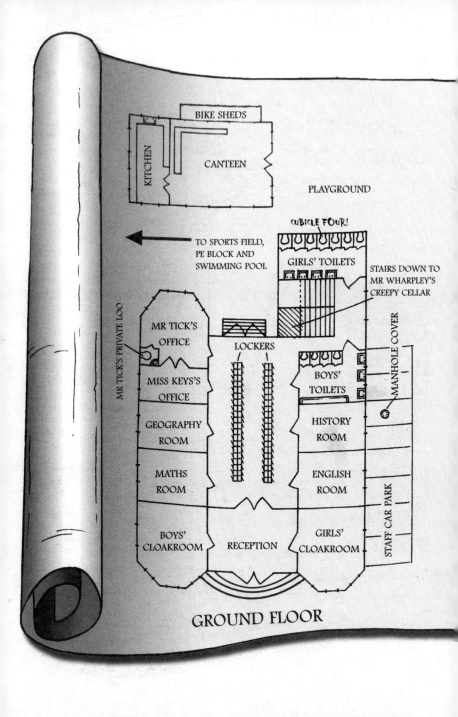

GROUND FLOOR

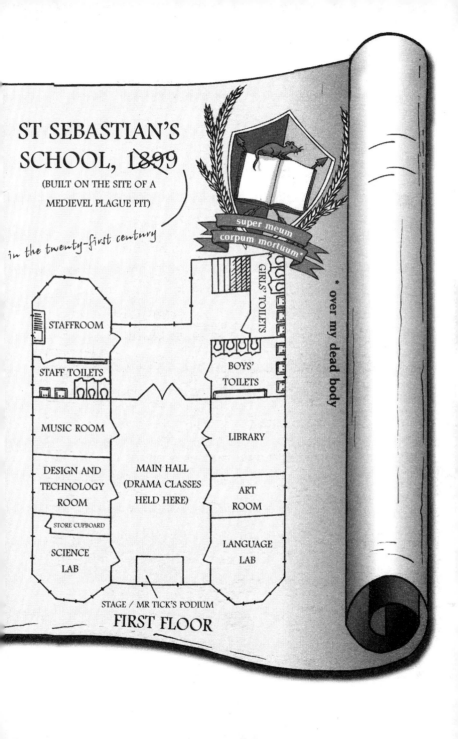

About the Black Death

The Black Death was a terrible plague that
is believed to have been spread by fleas on rats.
It swept through Europe in the fourteenth century,
arriving in England in 1348, where it killed
over one third of the population.

One of the Black Death's main symptoms was
**foul-smelling boils all over the body called
'buboes'.** The plague was so infectious that its
victims and their families were locked in their houses
until they died. Many villages were abandoned as
the disease wiped out their populations.

So many people died that graveyards overflowed
and bodies lay in the street, so special **'plague pits'**
were dug to bury the bodies. Almost every town
and village in England has a plague pit
somewhere underneath it, so watch out
when you're digging in the garden . . .

Dear Reader

As you may have already guessed, B. Strange is not a real name.

The author of this series is an ex-teacher who is currently employed by a little-known body called the Organisation For Spook Termination (Excluding Demons), or O.F.S.T.(E.D.). 'B. Strange' is the pen name chosen to protect his identity.

Together, we felt it was our duty to publish these books, in an attempt to save innocent lives. The stories are based on the author's experiences as an O.F.S.T.(E.D.) inspector in various schools over the past two decades.

Please read them carefully - you may regret it if you don't . . .

Yours sincerely
The Publisher.

PS - Should you wish to file a report on any suspicious supernatural occurrences at your school, visit **www.too-ghoul.com** and fill out the relevant form. We'll pass it on to O.F.S.T.(E.D.) for you.

PPS - All characters' names have been changed to protect the identity of the individuals. Any similarity to actual persons, living or undead, is purely coincidental.

CONTENTS

CHAPTER 1
TOILET TALES

'But I need to *go*!' Alexander wailed, dancing from foot to shiny-shoed foot. It was break time, and the corridors of St Sebastian's School were crammed with pupils. All the teachers were tucked safely away in the staffroom, slurping coffee.

'Well, go then, Stick! What's your problem?' asked James, pulling the sagging knot in his tie even looser.

'You know – girls!'

'Sorry – I don't get the connection. It's not one of your terrible jokes coming on, is it?'

'Looks like something'll be coming soon – a puddle!' sneered Gordon 'The Gorilla' Carver – the school bully – as he scooted past, clipping Alexander round the back of the head.

James glared after the bully as he ran down the corridor. 'Stick – I hate to say this, but The Gorilla has a point. You'd better go now!'

'But . . . it's all of these girls invading our conveniences. It's very *inconvenient!* You go

rushing in, unzipping your fly, and a girl's there doing girly stuff like brushing her manky hair or something – and she looks at you like you're the *contents* of the toilet instead of just being there because you need to use it . . .'
Alexander groaned.

'Well, you can't really blame them, you know,' said Lenny. 'There's only one set of girls' loos left for all the girls in the entire school while their ground-floor block is being rebuilt.'

At that moment, Leandra Maxwell, Lenny's sister, arrived. Stacey Carmichael, her best friend and the prettiest girl in school, trailed in her wake.

'New dance, Stick?' she honked. 'Very nice. Not sure it'll catch on though. Is it The Widdle Waltz? Or The Tinkle Tango?'

'It's not funny, Leandra!' growled Lenny. He shared his sister's dark curly hair and deep brown eyes, but that's where the similarities ended.

Leandra liked to tease. Her brother Lenny was the kindest person ever.

'You . . . you should keep out of our lavatories – it's against school rules!' Alexander blustered.

By now, a small crowd had begun to gather. Girls screeched with laughter and even a few boys were grinning. The Gorilla arrived, smelling trouble.

'Oh, yes – and *Daddy*'s the headmaster, isn't he? He'd be cross if we broke his precious rules, wouldn't he?' The Gorilla snarled, snapping a bubblegum bubble in Alexander's face. Even the sugary smell couldn't sweeten his mean expression. Lenny pushed the bully away.

'Leave him alone, Carver!'

'Who are you pushing about?' the bully blustered. 'If I could be bothered, I'd have you . . .' he sneered at Lenny. 'You're only friends with that loser,' he jabbed Alexander in the chest with a chubby finger, 'because you like hopeless cases!

4

I saw you, carrying that stupid hedgehog with scorched prickles you rescued last week.'

He turned to the crowd. 'He's got it in his locker, y'know. It smells, *and* it's full of fleas.' He turned back to Alexander and poked him in the shoulder. 'Yeah – just like you, Stick! And from the look of you, you're about to get even smellier!'

Alexander looked away.

Lenny got closer to Gordon. 'I said, leave . . . him . . . alone!' he growled.

Leandra stepped in between the boys.

A small girl tugged at Leandra's arm. 'Hey, you know, I wouldn't like to use the boys' toilets. I heard they were haunted . . .' she said. Leandra turned and frowned at the girl and she let go, smoothing the older girl's jumper sleeve. Continuing bravely, she added, 'Really. I heard that a kid went into that loo . . . and never came out again!'

'I heard that zombies ate him,' a boy grimaced horribly.

Stacey gave a pretty little shudder that made her short skirt twitch. It made a few of the boys twitch, too, like a chain reaction.

'Well, I heard there's an alien octopus that lives down the pipes. It eats poo – and year sevens!' a boy in year nine added.

'Naw . . . a headless horseman sweeps through the toilets banging on doors with his sword and slicing off legs at the ankles – knickers and all!' his friend called, swishing the air with an imaginary sabre as he spoke.

'Well,' Leandra said drily, 'I don't suppose many boys are sat there constipated with all that going on!' Stacey covered her mouth with her hand, her pink glossy nails sparkling as she tittered.

'I heard it was a portal for a dump demon,' said a tall year eight. 'It feeds off the gases in the toilets and suffocates people with its stinky breath as they sit on the throne. Its victims are doomed to haunt the toilet forever, wafting around on a cloud of methane . . .'

'From the stink coming out of the boys' toilets, I can believe *that* story!' laughed Leandra.

'I heard there's a vampire toilet seat in one of the cubicles,' another boy whispered. 'You sit down quite happily, but you notice that the seat's deathly cold. Just as it starts to warm up and you get comfy – CHOMP! Spiky gnashers clamp down on your bum. You're stuck there until every drop of your blood is drained – and you're dead!'

'Or should that be *undead*?' laughed another boy, sweeping his jacket over his shoulders like a vampire's cloak. Snapping his teeth at the crowd, he made a beeline for Stacey and her delicate pink neck. Leandra raised a hand in front of his face and the boy stopped dead. He melted into the crowd again.

'No – you're all wrong. It's a ghoul that hides in the shadows and snatches kids as they flush – and the noise hides their screams,' a small, worried boy said with a shudder.

'Actually, it's The Toilet Man,' a year-nine boy said, leaning against the wall. 'You say his name three times as you look in the mirror and your reflection slowly changes. Smoke swirls around your face and your eyes glint gold, like snake eyes. You bend closer to the mirror for a better look, rubbing it with your hand . . .' Everyone leant in as the boy told his tale.

'And The Toilet Man *grabs* it with his scaly talons and pulls you in!' he shouted, catching Stacey's hands and tugging her towards him. Everyone jumped.

'Well, that one's enough to make you wet yourself!' James laughed, suddenly reminded of Alexander's problem. He was now red in the face and quite obviously in pain, clutching the strap of his backpack so tightly that his knuckles were white.

'Come on, Stick,' Lenny whispered to his friend. 'While they're busy here, you can go to the loo undisturbed. I'll be your lookout and check for sneaky girls.' Alexander smiled gratefully. Lenny glowered at Gordon once more as they left.

'If only they all knew how close to the truth their stories are,' James sighed to himself as he made his way off down the corridor.

CHAPTER 2
AMPHITHEATRE ACTION

'This is *terrible!*' screeched Edith Codd, slamming
her skinny hand down on an upturned barrel
– or 'meeting table' as she liked to call it –
sending sludge and muck flying in all directions.
'I just can't *bear* this dreadful situation one
moment longer!'

Edith was the leader of the plague-pit ghosts,
a band of spirits that lived – or should that be
deaded? – in the sewer beneath St Sebastian's.
Edith hated the school with all her maggot-
infested heart.

Ambrose Harbottle slumped unhappily against a wall. He liked the sewer with its dank, festering walls complete with creepy inhabitants. He didn't want any changes to his cosy life. As Edith slapped her hand down again, a bulbous leech pinged off the side of the barrel and Ambrose caught it expertly, popping it into his mouth and chewing it noisily, like a thick wad of gum.

Above their heads, the rumble of hundreds of feet was beating out a rhythm. A strange whirring, grinding sound added to the noise and then an ear-splitting judder shook the sewer. Chunks of Victorian brickwork plopped into the sludge, startling a fat and rather lazy-looking rat. It chattered angrily and scampered away. Edith glared at the roof of the tunnel. She swept a layer of dust out of her stringy red hair and gritted her rotting teeth.

'I've had enough! They've gone too far this time . . .' Her rant was interrupted by a huge crash and she ran for cover under a heap of stained rags. There was a lull in the noise and Edith crept out again slowly. As one skinny leg, then another, and an arm appeared, William Scroggins was reminded of the big hairy spiders that lived behind the warm water pipes up in the school. Edith brushed herself off and smoothed her greasy skirt.

'As I was saying, before I was so rudely interrupted, I've had enough of this nonsense. The noise is *unbearable!* The floors of the school are creaking and groaning more than old mouldy breeches here . . .' she poked an elderly ghost rudely, '. . . and I half expect a gaggle of dreadful children to tumble through at any moment. The noise goes on all day. How is a girl ever expected to get her beauty sleep?' she simpered.

William started to laugh at the idea of Edith being beautiful, but managed to turn it into a hacking cough as her glare almost burnt a hole in his ectoplasm.

'We need to take immediate action. I'm calling an emergency meeting to get everyone involved. Ambrose, William – round everyone up!' She slammed her hand down on a pipe, which started to glow green.

Far above, in the school kitchen, a plughole belched and a cloud of stinking gas seeped into the room as two dinner ladies stood preparing lunch together.

'Sue, have you been stuffing yourself with that Baked Bean Surprise again?' asked Mrs Cooper

'What do you mean? I wouldn't eat that slop. It's only fit for kids!' said Mrs Meadows, stirring a huge vat of orange paste.

'Then what about the stench – where's that coming from if it's not you? It's certainly not me!' grumbled Mrs Cooper, wrinkling her nose. 'Are you poorly?'

'Don't you get cheeky with me, Lynn Cooper!' grumbled Mrs Meadows. She slapped her spoon down hard.

'Why are you in such a strop?'

'*Me?* Strop? It's *you* that's being nasty!'

'*Me?* Hardly! Now shift your fat backside – I need to get past.'

'*Me?* Fat? *That's* a laugh! We all know why there's never enough chocolate drops for the sponge pudding . . .'

'What are you saying?' growled Mrs Cooper.

'I'm past saying – now I'm *doing* . . .!' Mrs Meadows pushed Mrs Cooper against the table. She hit her elbow hard. Mrs Cooper picked up a handful of sticky rice and threw it at Mrs Meadows. Mrs Meadows flung a ladle of beans at Mrs Cooper and a full-scale food fight quickly erupted.

As the green glow on the pipe faded, they looked at each other, dripping with sauce. A blob of rice pudding slid down Mrs Meadows's cheek.

'Eh, Sue! What happened?' asked Mrs Cooper, wiping her friend's cheek.

'I don't know, Lynn, pet,' said Mrs Meadows, flicking a bean off her friend's shoulder. 'Let's put the kettle on before we clear up.'

Back in the sewer, Ambrose carried on trying to ignore Edith, picking a festering scab off his elbow and chewing it. William's forehead wrinkled almost as much as Edith's as he tried to think of an excuse to avoid getting involved in her plans.

'Go on, boy! Get a move on! This is an emergency!' She pushed William along the tunnel. 'Round everybody up now – you too, Ambrose! No slacking!'

William trudged off reluctantly. Cold drips of water plopped down his neck, making him shiver. He loved St Sebastian's and would do anything to keep it open. It made him feel as though he had friends. He loved to listen through the grille in the boys' toilets and hear the jokes the boys told, and the gales of laughter that followed. He had his favourites – James, Lenny and Alexander. William daydreamed about being part of their gang, and had imagined the nickname he would have. He liked 'Scroggers' . . .

'Scroggins! Are you daydreaming? This is important! Snap to it!' Edith Codd's voice sliced through William's daydreams. He jerked in fright and scuttled off into the darkness to tell the other ghosts about the meeting.

Gradually, the phantoms began to ooze out of the shadows, taking their places before Edith's furious face. She was waiting in the amphitheatre, the huge underground cavern constructed by the ghosts in the sewer over the last six centuries.

Lady Grimes wafted in elegantly, dressed in velvets and furs. Bertram Ruttle danced along, playing a small bone xylophone that was strung on a cord of gristle round his neck.

Edith called the plague-pit ghosts to order. 'I have summoned you all to discuss the disturbances. It's time to take action! I'm sure you all agree. Rest in peace? Not a chance with all those dreadful children clattering about. And, as if that wasn't enough, there are now those horrid machines bellowing out noise at all hours . . .'

'It's enough to wake the dead!' Ambrose chuckled.

A few ghosts laughed heartily, despite Edith's glares. Lady Grimes giggled and Ambrose smiled at her, warmly. 'Hello, pretty lady . . .' he smarmed, sliding towards her.

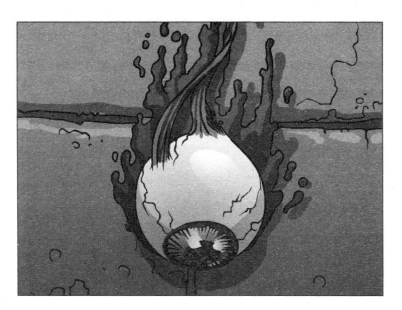

Edith whacked him so hard from behind that his ectoplasm exploded and, for one awful moment, his head was smeared all over the walls. One of his eyes looked startled as it slid over a clump of mould and wedged there. As the wisps slid back into place, Ambrose's face reappeared, looking sheepish.

'As I was saying,' Edith frowned at Ambrose, 'we need a plan of action. Does anyone have any ideas?'

Suddenly, the sewer was quieter than the grave. Even the Howling Haunt fell silent. Bertram stopped playing his xylophone. William stared down, suddenly incredibly interested in a clump of grot floating by. He was afraid to say anything in case he helped Edith – and that was the last thing he wanted to do. St Sebastian's was his lifeline – or at least, his *afterlife* line. Ambrose was gazing at some juicy leeches throbbing on his boot.

The drip of stinky water was the only sound. Edith stared around her furiously, but no one would meet her eye.

'I see. It's up to me, as usual,' she said, coldly. 'I might have known, you spineless spooks!' And she stormed off, leaving flakes of skin drifting in her wake.

William could feel an empty space deep in his chest. He was afraid that Edith would finally get her way and St Sebastian's would close. He had an idea. Perhaps if he agreed to 'help' Edith, he could keep an eye on her and scupper her plans.

'Edith . . . wait! I'll help you!' he called. His voice echoed away from him and got lost in the warren of tunnels. 'Ambrose – if we go along with her, we might find a way to mess up her plans!' William whispered.

'Aye, lad . . . I suppose you're right. Edith! Wait for us!' He heaved himself upright with a creak of non-existent bones. Plucking a juicy leech from a clump of sludge that was sprouting mouldy green hair, he held it up to his watery eyes and smiled. 'Come on, my beauty! Down the hatch!' He sucked in the leech with his gummy lips as though it were a strand of rubbery spaghetti. With a soft 'plop', his lips smacked together and the leech was gone.

'Ah, it's the small pleasures that make the afterlife worth living,' sighed Ambrose. Thinking of the lovely Lady Grimes, he trailed after William.

Like a ghostly Hansel and Gretel, the pair followed the trail of Edith's skin flakes into the darkness.

CHAPTER 3
JAMES SIMPSON: SPECIAL AGENT

The bell rang for break. Alexander needed the loo again. 'I can't understand why the builders are taking so incredibly long!' he moaned.

'I've been wondering, you don't think the builders are in league with the ghosts, do you?' said James. 'There's a lot of noise and a layer of dust on everything from the windowsills to the drinks machine, but they don't seem to be getting anywhere. It's a bit fishy, if you ask me!'

23

'I don't know about that, but I do know that I can't stand this much longer!' grumbled Alexander.

'I know what you mean. I have enough fights with Leandra at home about using the bathroom. She's in there for hours soaking in the bath – and it always seems to be when I'm desperate! She runs the tap, too, so I have to listen to the trickling noise . . .' moaned Lenny.

'Blimey! I'm glad I don't have a sister!' Alexander shuddered.

'And how on *earth* could the builders be in league with the ghosts? I'm sure Mr Tick didn't look up their number in the *Phantom Phonebook*!' laughed Lenny.

'It wasn't Dad who hired them. It was that Mr Welk, the Chair of Governors,' said Alexander. 'I've never trusted that man . . . he smiles all the time. It never reaches his eyes, though . . . and there are always bits of food in his moustache – yuck!'

'What if the ghosts have *possessed* them?' asked James. 'I saw a film like that once. Has anybody seen their heads spinning, or heard them talking in weird voices?' He was smiling, but his eyes were wide, so Alexander wasn't quite sure if he was joking.

'Tell you what – I'll sneak down the corridor and see what's happening. It might be nothing.'

James sidled down the corridor, scuttling from doorway to doorway. The corridor was quiet because everyone was outside. A faint smell of the day's school dinner wafted in from the canteen, masking the stale odour of dust that was everywhere now the builders had started work.

A low murmuring came from the staffroom, punctuated by Mr Watts coughing. James smiled as he remembered the sight of Mr Watts doing just that during this morning's science lesson, blowing a cloud of carefully arranged crystals halfway across the lab.

He slithered behind a large but rather wilted rubber plant that stood next to the door, peering round the door jamb to try and catch sight of the builders. He could see a cluster of them around the kettle. The nearest builder's belly bulged over the straining waistband of his dusty jeans. He scratched his backside and then used the same hand to rummage about in the box of teabags.

James shuddered.

Ms Legg, the PE teacher, sat staring out of the window towards the football pitch. James shot backwards as she turned her head towards the door – and directly at him. He was safe though – all she was interested in was the youngest builder's biceps.

The soupy smell of instant noodles seeped out of the doorway and caught in James's throat. No wonder the building work was taking so long – the only thing the builders were busy with was the kettle!

James slid away from the staffroom and went to the downstairs girls' toilets to look for signs of progress while all the builders were otherwise occupied. If there was anything spooky going on, he'd find out!

As he came round the corner, he heard banging coming from the toilets. His fists clenched and his scalp tightened – but he had to see what was making that noise. He pushed the doors opened and peered inside.

What he saw was horrific. It made his breath hiss between his teeth.

In front of him was a huge, hairy builder's bum poking above a straining belt that threatened to give up the battle at any moment. The builder was hunched over a tangle of rusty pipes in the corner of the room.

James pushed the door open wide. The builder straightened up and rubbed his back. He caught sight of James in the mirror and jumped.

27

'Blimey! I wasn't expecting to see anyone there – you made me jump out of my skin!' He started to cough. As he rumbled to a halt, he pushed his hat back on his head.

'Problems?' asked James.

'You could say that! This old Victorian pipe work is a nightmare. The joints are rusted rigid and there's no order to it at all – it's just a mess. We'll have to get a plumbing squad in now. That could take weeks!' He gave his bum a thoughtful scratch. 'But they've got to come out. They're dangerous.'

James felt the blood rush away from his face and pool in his boots, leaving him light-headed. *Dangerous? Come out?* The builders *did* know about the ghosts then! He stared with wide eyes at the man as he rubbed his hands clean on an old rag pulled from his back pocket.

'Hey – are you all right, son? You look like you've seen a ghost!' James's eyes bulged out of his head. The man put a hand on the boy's shoulder and James flinched.

'Are you poorly? Shall I take you to the nurse?' the builder fussed. 'It's a bit pongy in here – did it make you feel sick? Sorry, son. It's just that these pipes are dangerous and they have to come out. I know, it's making the place stink . . .'

'Pipes . . .? Pipes! Of *course*, the pipes!' James's face flushed red. The builder looked at him as though he was stupid.

'Let's get you some fresh air,' said the builder, helping James out of the toilets and out into the passageway.

James bent forwards, and rested his hands on his thighs. He took some deep gulps of air and hiccupped with laughter. 'I'll be fine, thanks. It was just the smell – thanks again!'

James rushed away. The builder stared after him, scratching his head, but he soon forgot all about him as the young builder arrived carrying a mug of steaming tea and a chocolate biscuit.

James found Alexander and Lenny waiting in the playground.

'Good news! It's not ghost activity – it's tea breaks! Those toilets will never be finished at this rate. I've just seen the builders lazing about in the staffroom stuffing their faces,' James reported.

Lenny nodded. Alexander just looked pained. He needed the loo again and couldn't face battling through another line of giggling girls.

'I can't bear it! Yesterday was the worst yet. I wanted to go before PE, but there were loads of girls about. By the time the match had finished, I was bursting. I ran all the way from the field, and I was bending down and tugging at my boots as I ran. I jumped up, kicked my boots off and barged straight into Stacey. I was sweaty; she was cool and calm – even though I'd nearly knocked her over. I said sorry and dived into a cubicle. To make things worse, Leandra came into the toilets and I had to listen to Stacey telling her what had happened!'

'Impressive,' smiled Lenny.

'Never mind that,' said James. 'Listen, even though we haven't seen anything suspicious yet, I still think we should keep an eye on those toilets, just in case. You never know . . .'

In a corner of the playground, a small girl squealed as the drinking fountain squirted green slime in her eye when she bent to drink. In the

staffroom, terrible gurgling noises chugged under the sink, startling Mr Tick, the headmaster. And when Mr Wharpley, the caretaker, filled his bucket from a tap in the cellar he found it was full of slimy leeches.

The ghosts were restless. Trouble was on its way.

CHAPTER 4
THE LITTLE COCKROACH THAT COULD

Edith paced up and down. She scratched absent-
mindedly at her head, flakes of skin and dandruff
sailing into the air. She was frowning so deeply
that her eyebrows threatened to meet her lips.
'I need to think of a way to control those awful
men – the ones with the noisy machines . . . but
how? Think, Edith, think . . .' she grumbled.

She slumped on to a ledge, leaning her head
back and closing her eyes. She sighed deeply.

A cockroach scuttled up the wall next to Edith's face. She heard the scratching, opened her eyes and slapped hard, denting the sludge as she tried to squash the shiny, brown bug.

The roach hissed and dropped to the floor. It shook its mangled feelers angrily at Edith and started to climb the wall again. It found the dent she had made in the wall and settled down to lay its eggs.

'That's *it*!' Edith screeched, startling an elderly ghost so badly that he shot up a pipe and ended up in the science lab. 'Clever beetle!' she purred, stroking the rubbery creature with a scabby finger. The roach flicked its legs at her angrily. 'Ambrose! We must all be like this beetle!'

Ambrose stopped stroking Lady Grimes's hair and turned to Edith. 'What? Live in a sewer and burrow in sludge? Some of us enjoy that already . . .' he said as he dug a leech out of the wall with a grimy fingernail.

'No, you stupid man! This wonderful creature refused to give up on its quest to climb the wall. It turned a problem into a gift. Look at it, nesting in the dent already . . .' she cooed at the roach like a film star with a tiny dog in a handbag.

She picked the roach up and it squirted foul liquid at her face. 'Isn't he wonderful, William?' she asked.

Edith's strange behaviour was making William uneasy. 'Er . . . yes . . .?' he said.

Edith raised a hand to sweep her greasy hair out of her eyes and William flinched. Edith didn't notice. She was still staring at the beetle.

'I've got it!' she suddenly squealed.

'I'm sure you have . . . but is it catching?' Ambrose whispered into Lady Grimes's ear. She tittered and Edith turned to look at them.

'Yes, it is good news, isn't it?' she smiled, her eyes lighting up with eerie, red flames. William shuddered. What *was* she planning?

'I shall not give up. Just like this brave little beetle here.' She stroked the roach again. It bit a chunk out of her festering finger, then realised its mistake and spat it out again quickly. Edith was so far in to her rant that she didn't even notice. Wisps of ectoplasm wafted out of the hole in her finger and William stared, fascinated, as it curled away like smoke.

'And, just like this fine beetle, I shall take the situation and use it to my advantage!' she cackled wildly. Somewhere above Edith's head, a toilet flushed.

A year-nine girl froze as she was pulling up her tights. Could that have been laughter coming from the toilet? She shook her head and rubbed her eyes. She was working too hard for her SATs ... that must be it.

As girl began to wash her hands, a gurgling came from the pipes. Black sludge squirted out of the tap and she ran screaming from the toilets.

'Edith ... what did you have in mind?' William asked, politely. He needed to know exactly what her plans were so he could spoil them.

'Ah, William ... thank you for asking!'

Edith trilled. She stretched her mouth into a horrible grin.

William saw her stained teeth glistening as her slimy, grey tongue slid over them. A vein was throbbing in her neck. It looked like a big, pink slug slithering towards the darkness of her collar. He felt his mouth go dry. The vein only appeared when Edith was very, very excited – and that always meant trouble for someone. Usually him.

'Those builders are constantly in the room where the water is heated to make drinks. We can take advantage of that fact. Some of us can slide up the pipes and into the tap, whereupon we shall slip into the water they use to make the tea . . . and there you have it!'

'Have *what*?' William asked, his face screwed up with the effort of trying to understand Edith's idea.

Ambrose had already given up and was snoring gently, propped up against the wall. A single leech had attached itself to his nostril, waving in the air like a black ribbon each time he breathed out.

'Is *everyone* here stupid?' Edith roared, all traces of her good mood gone. Ambrose woke with a start, snorting the leech straight up his nose. He swallowed and smiled.

'Let me explain – *again*! We get into their tea and then, in one slurp, we end up in their bellies.' She smiled for a third time and William stepped back quickly.

'But – how does that help us, Edith?' he asked.

Edith bent in close to William's face. He could see the flakes of skin on her cheeks rising as she breathed. Tiny insects crawled out of her hairline, then saw her face and thought better of it, running for cover in her eyebrows.

'POSSESSION!' she bellowed.

William flew up into the air and banged his head on a stone jutting out of the wall. Hundreds of spectres scattered in fright. Ambrose was so startled he dropped his pot of leeches and the creatures crawled away to safety.

'Possession?' asked William, rubbing his head. 'What do you mean?'

'We enter the builders . . . and take control!' Edith cackled wildly, flecks of spittle flying from her rubbery lips. William gulped.

'I don't think I'll manage that . . . it sounds really hard . . . it might even be hard for you.'

'Oh, don't be stupid! It's not hard at all! I'll show you what Edith Codd can do!' She swept over to the pipes, plucked out a dead rat and a tangle of hair from the end of one of them and began to push herself into the opening.

First she forced in her feet, then (with a push) her saggy bottom. With a heave, she pushed herself in further until all anyone could see was her head. Her eyes bulged with the pressure.

Finally, with a soft 'plop', like a snot bubble bursting, she was gone.

CHAPTER 5
OOPS–SPLATTERFINGERS!

The boys were hanging about in the
playground, waiting for their call into the
canteen. Sweet wrappers and crisp packets blew
about, evidence of brave attempts to fill stomachs
before they were tortured with school–dinner
slop. The food at St Sebastian's varied by
name, but not much by taste. It was all grim
and greasy.

Lenny, James and Alexander were looking
at the brightly coloured menu taped to the
noticeboard.

'Look! It says "Hotpot Surprise" today. Do you think it's yesterday's mince, reheated?' groaned James in disgust.

'The surprise will be if it's edible!' laughed Alexander, weakly.

'I took some of that mince home yesterday for my hedgehog. Even he wouldn't eat it – and he eats slugs!' agreed Lenny.

'Talking of slow-moving things, I still think we should keep a close eye on those builders. We could go and have another look after lunch. I know I didn't see anything suspicious last time, but I've got a bad feeling about all of this,' said James.

'You're right. I know that builder seemed normal enough, but you never know with adults. One minute they're nice as pie; the next thing you're grounded,' grumbled Lenny.

'I can tell you've met my dad, then!' laughed Alexander. James grabbed him round the neck with his arm and scrubbed his head with his knuckles, only to be pounced on by Ms Legg.

She gave James a lecture on aggressive behaviour, but her words just faded into general teacher droning.

'But it was a joke!' James moaned, looking up to discover that he was talking to Ms Legg's back as she swept through the double doors into the main school.

'Don't worry about it, James. Dad was complaining about having to go to anti-bully training last night so the teachers will be looking for it everywhere . . . for today, at any rate.'

'Talk of the devil . . .' murmured Lenny. Gordon Carver had lumbered over and punched the top of James's arm.

'Didn't know you had it in you, Simpson! A bully, eh? Now you've brushed off those geeks, you can come and sit with us at dinner if you like . . .'

'Erm . . . t–thanks . . .' stuttered James. 'I mean . . . No! I wasn't bullying him . . . I was just messing about . . .'

'Oh, I understand!' Gordon said, cracking a hideous grin and tapping the side of his nose with his finger. '"Just messing about", yeah, I use that one all the time!' He roared with laughter and several of the smaller boys ran and hid behind the bike sheds. 'See you later!' he called and trundled off, snarling at another year-eight kid who had the cheek to be standing in his way.

After lunch, the boys made their way to what was left of the ground-floor girls' toilet block. One of the walls was reduced to rubble and the site was screened from the playground by a rough wooden frame covered by plastic sheeting. The plastic wafted backwards and forwards like a ghost, reaching towards the boys as they stood staring at it.

'Blimey – it's like a war zone!' said James. Their feet were leaving tracks in the thick, grimy layer of dust that covered the ground.

'That plastic looks like a quarantine curtain to stop infection,' laughed Alexander nervously.

'It could be,' said James. 'St Sebastian's *was* built on a plague pit, remember?'

'Yes, but the plague was wiped out in Europe in the nineteenth century, silly!' said Alexander. 'I don't think we should go in if it's taped off, though. There must be a logical reason for all that plastic being there . . .'

The boys looked at each other, unsure of what to do next.

'What's that noise?' James asked.

Alexander jumped. 'What noise? Ghostly noises?'

'No – wait – I can hear it too!' said Lenny. 'It's a scratching noise . . .' He moved closer to the plastic sheeting. 'It's coming from these folds of plastic . . .'

'Careful!' shouted Alexander, making Lenny jump and fall against the plastic sheeting. He tangled in the material as he went down and it slithered to the floor, pulled free of the tape holding it up.

A small, grey mouse popped out of a fold of plastic and hopped on to Lenny's stomach. Then it ran up his chest and peered at his face. Liking what it saw, it settled down to sleep in his collar.

'Here's the source of the noise!' laughed Lenny, cupping the mouse gently in his hands. He popped it in his pocket.

'Well, now the plastic's down, we may as well have a quick look,' said James, stepping into what was left of the toilet block. Lenny and Alexander sighed and got behind him.

The toilets were missing and a layer of water bubbled up through one of the holes. It was mixing with the dust to make slick, black paste that stuck to their feet.

'There's only one builder in there again — the same bloke I spoke to last time,' James whispered.

'James . . . I think he's talking to himself . . .' Alexander hissed.

The boys edged closer. The builder was bent over an open pipe, muttering into the open end.

Suddenly, his head snapped round to face the boys. His eyes widened and he jumped to his feet. He rocked backwards and forwards a bit.

Lenny put out a hand to steady him and the builder's meaty hand shot past him and grabbed a sledgehammer. He swung the hammer behind him and rocked back on his heels. Swinging wildly, he smashed lumps out of the wall, whistling tunelessly between his teeth. The toilets filled with brick dust and cement powder.

The boys started to choke and splutter. James waved them closer so they could hear him over the noise. 'This is weird – he was really friendly last time. He's almost acting as if we aren't here . . . I'll see if he remembers me.'

He walked forwards carefully, standing to the side to avoid the swinging hammer. 'Excuse me! Excuse me, sir . . .'

The builder didn't look round. James tried again.

'How's it going? It's me – I was in here before . . .'

'Fine, fine,' the builder grunted. 'No problems. You run along now and let me get on.'

He carried on swinging. Then he dropped the sledgehammer and picked up a small, vicious-looking club hammer and smashed it into the bricks. Sharp pieces flew everywhere.

Then, with one extra-wild swing, he accidentally smashed the heavy hammer hard down on to his hand.

'Oh, no! That's gotta hurt! Are you OK?' called Lenny.

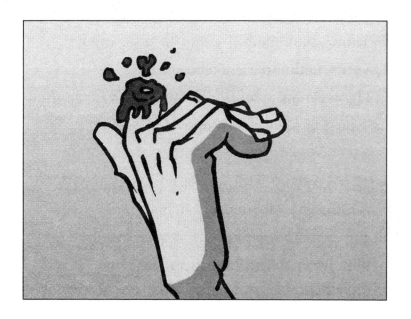

The boys stared on in horror. The builder, however, carried on hammering, not noticing that one of his fingers had been smashed off. It looked like a squashed sausage as it rolled down into a pile of rubble. Green goo dripped on to the plaster dust below, making the handle of the hammer wet.

'That's scientifically impossible!' Alexander cried, stunned.

'I think I'm going to hurl!' James gasped.

'Here, let me help . . .' said Lenny, walking towards the builder.

The man dropped the hammer with a clunk and lunged towards Alexander. 'You! You nosy boys . . . I'll sort you out once and for all!' His face twisted with anger, and his dripping hand grasped Alexander, leaving green smears on his gleaming white shirt. He shook the headmaster's son so hard that his teeth chattered together.

'He's not a builder – he's a ghost!' shouted James. He sprung after the sledgehammer and snatched it up, ready to rescue his friend.

'T-t-thanks, James,' juddered Alexander, 'I'd m-m-managed to c-come to that c-c-conclusion myself!'

Lenny kicked the ghost's shin and there was a sickening crunch.

James swung the hammer but, in trying to avoid Alexander, he swung wide and missed.

Suddenly, the toilet door slammed open against the wall.

'What on *earth's* going on in here?' demanded a voice. It was Mr Wharpley, the caretaker. His eyes goggled as he took in the scene before him.

The boys froze. With the dripping goo and swinging weapons, it was like a scene from one of James's computer games. But this time, the fighting was for real.

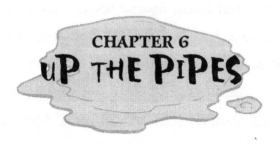

CHAPTER 6
UP THE PIPES

William stared at the pipe. He frowned and tapped it thoughtfully with his fingers.

'She's a mad old bird, that one,' said Ambrose, picking his teeth with an old cotton bud he'd found in the sewer. 'She'll not rest until she has her own way.' He jiggled the makeshift toothpick inside one of his ears, dislodging a curious spider.

'Well, I thought we'd have a bit of time to think after Edith disappeared, but she's just whispered to me down the pipe from the girls' toilet block. She wants us to follow her and help her to take over the school! What are we going to do, Ambrose?'

'We're going to go up top for a look, my lad!' Ambrose grunted as he pulled himself to his feet. 'Where is she now and what's she doing?'

'Well, actually it sounded quite funny,' William whispered, looking over his shoulder. 'She made it to the staffroom exactly as planned but, just as she was oozing out of the tap into the boiler, one of the builders spotted her. She said they all screamed and ran away, getting jammed in the door as they fought to get out. They left noodles and tea all over the place. The caretaker was furious when he saw the mess!'

'I would have loved to have seen that!' choked Ambrose. When he continued to choke and went a bit red, William patted him on the back. Ambrose cleared his throat and spat a blob of glowing ectoplasm on the floor. 'Thanks, lad. You're a good 'un!'

'But you'll never guess what she did next – she morphed in to one of the builders. Just imagine – Edith, in baggy jeans!'

The two ghosts held on to each other and laughed until they were gasping.

'Ooh! My poor old ribs . . . I haven't laughed that hard for a century!' chuckled Ambrose. 'Seriously though, boy,' he said, sobering up, 'morphing takes every drop of energy a ghost has. It makes you fade horribly. Last time I did it, I was flicking in and out like a candle flame in a hurricane. It's just not possible to hold another shape like that for a long time.'

'Imagine if Edith faded away completely . . .' William sighed.

Both ghosts were silent for a moment.

'Aye, well, lad – there's no point in daydreaming. We all have our burden to bear, and Edith is ours.' He patted William on the shoulder. 'Don't worry. Even that mean woman, full of fury as she is, can't see off the entire school single-handed. Tell you what, though, I'd give a lot to see her all dressed up as a builder. What do you say we ooze up the pipes ourselves and take a peep?'

'Well, it would be fun . . . and I want to make sure she doesn't do anything to hurt my friends. If we went up there we could try to mess up Edith's plans. And I'd love to see Edith as a builder, too!' chuckled William.

'Well, let's see what we can do about getting up that pipe, for starters,' nodded Ambrose.

William eyed the end of the pipe, then Ambrose's large rear end. How would he manage?

'I know what you're thinking, lad – I'm a well-built figure of a man. But remember, ectoplasm stretches.' He started to force himself into the pipe, head first. He pulled his head out again with a popping noise and then turned to William.

A leech danced happily on his balding head. 'Follow me, son,' he said and began to disappear up the pipe.

After his head, his shoulders followed. William could hear grunting and wheezing as Ambrose edged further into the pipe. There was a nasty moment when his wobbly belly got jammed and William heard muffled cursing. He stepped up behind Ambrose and pushed his skinny shoulder under his friend's backside.

That did the trick. With a heave, a gassy noise and a cloud of unpleasant wind, Ambrose disappeared.

William could hear grunting and a series of small explosions of air as Ambrose made his way up the pipe. He put his head into the pipe and pulled it back sharply, scrubbing at his nose with his hand. This was going to be a smelly job. 'Ambrose, I wish you'd gone up the pipe feet first, like Edith . . .'

William found an old rag and tied it round his nose and mouth. He took one last look round the gloomy sewer and pushed his head into the pipe. The sulphurous stench Ambrose had left behind almost choked him. *At least I won't get lost . . .!* William thought, pushing himself into the pipe.

Once inside, his progress was much easier than Ambrose's because he was so skinny. In the darkness, he felt spongy muck press against him.

The walls of the pipe had furred up over the years, making the space inside narrow and rough. William scraped his knee on a jagged lump. 'Good job ghosts don't feel pain!' he comforted himself.

As he wriggled up the pipe, he could hear Ambrose struggling along in front of him. From time to time, clouds of gas that made him gag came rumbling back down it, hitting his face with sour warmth. 'Sorry!' Ambrose's voice floated back. William winced. He scrubbed at his nose again. It was going to be a long, long journey.

Finally, they reached the toilet block. Ambrose and William oozed out of the pipe. Edith was standing nearby.

'Oh, what can I *do*? I've been attacked by hooligans!' she wailed. 'Who would attack a *lady* like me? Oh, the dreadful children!'

Edith had completely forgotten that she didn't look like a lady at all. She'd adopted a builder's form – complete with wobbly belly and hairy bum. She started to rock backwards and forwards. 'They've worked out who I am . . . but I can't let them get the better of me! What to do, oh, what to do . . .'

William and Ambrose just stared – first at Edith, then at each other. Ambrose shrugged. He pointed at Edith. 'We need to look like that, son.'

William concentrated hard. He struggled and wriggled as he tried to change himself. 'This is hard, Ambrose!' he whispered.

Edith continued to moan and groan and didn't notice them at all.

Ambrose was having trouble too. 'Aye, lad – it is that!' he groaned. He strained extra hard and a foul smell filled the air. 'Sorry!' Ambrose chuckled.

At last, William felt himself start to change. He imagined a picture he'd seen in an old magazine left in the PE changing rooms. It showed a boy wearing a black top with swirly writing and pictures of skulls on it. Soon, he was wearing the same top.

'Hey, you're good at this!' Ambrose whispered. He was developing a beer belly, stubble and greying hair.

William felt his neck, which was strange and solid. He stretched his fingers and shook his legs

at the ankle. He looked at himself in the mirror and smiled. 'I think this is going to be fun, Ambrose!' he said.

Meanwhile, Edith was pacing up and down by the cubicles, muttering to herself. Drips of green ectoplasm splashed on to the tiles below, spreading to make a dark stain. A spider scuttled closer to take a look and squealed as the hairs on its legs were singed where they touched the goo. It limped away to hide under an old, dry bar of soap. Edith closed her eyes and sank to the floor.

'Where *are* those stupid ghosts? They'll not be much help, but needs must. Oh, what to do? What to do . . .' Edith started to panic.

She flapped her hand up to her face and patted her hair. She jumped in fright when she felt a woollen hat on her head – and until she remembered she was builder-shaped. Then she felt something crawl across her face where her hand was fluttering and realised she was leaking ectoplasm where she'd smashed off a finger.

Edith looked around on the rubbly floor for the missing digit and discovered it had already dissolved into a pool of glowing green sludge. A fly was drowning in it and Edith flicked at it with her boot.

'This is terrible! Those horrid children know who I am . . . and I can't stay like this for much longer . . . it's such a strain.' She groaned and leant against the tiled wall, closing her eyes and raising her hand to her forehead.

Her hand seemed to sink through the builder's face, which wavered like a reflection on water disturbed by a breeze. She massaged her own flaky forehead that lurked there under the surface. 'What to do . . . what to do . . . everything is ruined! Where *are* those stupid ghosts? I can't trust them with anything when I'm not around! My plans are a mess . . . No, stay calm, Edith – you can do this! You haven't come this far to be defeated by three silly little boys . . .'

A polite cough startled her from own pep talk. She jumped and gave a rather girlish squeal for a burly builder. Her eyes opened wide as she saw that the cough belonged to a man. There were two of them, standing looking directly at her. Builders!

'Erm . . . is t-tea break over already, lads?' Edith stammered. 'Did you bring me back a biscuit?' The builders smiled at her like idiots. The smaller one even giggled. That gave it away – she would have recognised that stupid snigger anywhere.

'William? Ambrose? Thank goodness it's you!' she slithered back against the wall. 'I mean – at long last! Where have you been, you *ridiculous* ghosts? Leaving me waiting like that! What were you *thinking*?'

The ghosts looked at one another. Ambrose had morphed into a tall builder with greying hair and a large beer belly that wobbled above his belt. Edith noticed with a shudder that he was wearing a gold hoop earring. Ambrose flicked the earring gently with a meaty finger.

'You like it, Edith?' he smiled, exposing tea-stained teeth.

'Most certainly *not*! It looks ridiculous, you silly man!'

'I thought it made me look a bit like a pirate, you know? I always fancied running off to sea. And I heard that some of those builders had earrings – Lady Grimes told me.'

'Shut UP!' Edith shouted, now quite recovered. Ambrose frowned, but kept quiet. Edith looked at William.

He had morphed into a teenaged apprentice builder. He wore jeans and a rock-band T-shirt with a skull on the front.

Edith poked the skull on the shirt. 'I suppose you thought this was funny . . .? No respect, youngsters. Dreadful!' she sniffed. 'You're not very good at this, are you? I mean, *I* look convincing. Who are you two going to fool, with that dreadful purple tinge to your skin and the red, glowing eyes? Pathetic.' Edith snorted.

'Well, she seemed pretty convinced when we first appeared, judging by that squeal . . .' Ambrose whispered to William.

'What was that?' hissed Edith. 'I thought I told you to SHUT UP! Anyway, now on to stage two of my plan.'

'But you said your plans were ruined,' William said, hopefully. 'That's what you were talking about when we arrived . . .'

Edith's mouth opened and closed like a fish that had been flushed down a toilet. Her face darkened and Ambrose took a step backwards. William flinched as she stepped closer and bent her face towards his. 'It's a good job you're dead already, Scroggins . . .' she hissed, pushing him sharply with her stubby fingers.

William staggered, not yet in control of his morphed legs. Ambrose reached out a hand and steadied him.

Edith paced backwards and forwards across the dusty floor, kicking rubble out of her way with a boot as she passed.

'Looks like she's not in the mood for obstacles!' Ambrose whispered.

William didn't dare show that he had even heard.

'As I was saying,' Edith snarled, 'now for the next stage of my plan.'

CHAPTER 7
A SMASHING TIME

Mr Tick was admiring his reflection in the brass nameplate on his desk. It looked just like a smaller version of the nameplate on his door, but this one was as shiny as a mirror.

He straightened up and flicked some imaginary fluff off his sleeve, then smiled to himself as he started a fresh game of solitaire on his computer, whistling a happy little tune through his teeth.

He paused and gazed out the window, lord of all he could see — but his smiled slipped as he spotted Mr Wharpley marching towards him.

Oh, no – pupils! he shuddered silently. He shuffled his papers into busy-looking piles on his desk. There was a rap on his door and Mr Wharpley's shape appeared through the frosted glass.

'Enter . . .' the headmaster sighed, leaning back in his leather chair.

The caretaker snaked his head around the door. 'I have, ahem, some horrible little yobs from year seven here, sir. One of them, I'm afraid to say,' he smiled broadly 'is your son.'

Mr Tick shot forwards, his chair skidding across the wooden floor. 'My son? Bring the boys in here straight away, before somebody sees!' he hissed. Mr Wharpley pushed the boys into the room.

They stood in front of the desk – but knew better than to stand on the expensive rug that lay in front of it. Mr Wharpley stood with his legs apart and his arms crossed. He was smiling.

'I heard a terrible noise coming from the toilets – the *out of bounds toilets*, I might add.'

Mr Wharpley pursed his lips. 'They were attacking one of the builders – with his own tools! I blame them computer games, I do . . .' His head bobbed up and down as he spoke, as though he were agreeing with himself.

'*What?* You did WHAT?' the headmaster bellowed at the boys. They shuffled and looked at each other. The caretaker had marched them up here so quickly that they hadn't had a chance to get their story straight.

'As I said, Mr Tick . . .' Mr Wharpley began.

'You may go now. Thank you,' the headmaster said, tight-lipped.

'But I was just going to say . . .' the caretaker continued.

'I said you may GO, Mr Wharpley. There must be a floor somewhere around here that needs mopping!'

The caretaker's jaw swung open. 'But I thought you'd want . . .'

'NOW!' Mr Tick roared, a vein in his forehead pulsing. He fixed the man with a glare he normally reserved for pupils in detention.

'I'll . . . I have to, er . . . yes, of course, sir. Thank you, Mr Tick, sir,' Mr Wharpley mumbled as he backed away towards the door. He waved a hand behind him, feeling for the handle. When he found it, he turned and fled.

Mr Tick stared at the boys. 'Well?' he asked.

Alexander cleared his throat and looked at his dad. His mouth opened and closed a couple of times, then he lowered his eyes to the floor. Lenny looked straight ahead out of the window. James glanced at his friends and then at Mr Tick.

'We were just . . . we heard . . .' he swallowed hard and hung his head.

Alexander took a deep breath. 'Dad . . . we weren't attacking anyone, we were defend –'

'*Dad?* Alexander, must I remind you once *again* of the nine o'clock to three-twenty rule? That

70

I am "Mr Tick" or "headmaster" or "sir" between those times . . .' He sighed heavily.

Suddenly, they all heard shouting and banging coming from the playground and Alexander's reply was drowned out by what sounded like arguing and shrieking.

Mr Tick jumped up and rushed to the window to find out what was going on. The boys looked at each other, then followed suit.

A cloud of dust filled the playground and the builders appeared to be fighting with the machines – and each other.

'Have they gone mad . . .?' muttered Mr Tick, running from the room. 'Miss Keys! Ring the police! I'm not having this sort of disturbance at my school!' he shouted.

He ran back into the room. 'Boys – back to your classrooms. Alexander, I shall deal with you later – at home!' he glared. He returned to stare out of the window once more.

The boys headed to the rear doors leading out on to the playground for a better view.

'Look at that builder holding on to the cement mixer!' said James.

As the dust cleared, they could see the outline of the builder they'd been fighting with.

'And there are two more!' said Lenny.

'D'you notice anything special about them, guys?' asked James.

The boys looked closely. Alexander rubbed the grimy window carefully with a clean hankie and Lenny pressed his face against the glass.

'They . . . they're . . . glowing!' Lenny breathed. The cold glass fogged in front of him.

'*Exactly,*' nodded James.

'So they're ghosts, too?' asked Alexander.

'They must be. This must be a plan to get rid of us all!' said James. 'We have to find a way to stop them!'

Lenny and Alexander looked from James to each other and back to James again.

'But how?' Alexander said.

CHAPTER 8
ACTION STATIONS!

'I've decided we need to use the tools that have been made available to us – so get on with it,' Edith said, firmly.

William and Ambrose stared at Edith. They were totally baffled. 'Oh, of course, I need to spell it out to you two idiots . . .' she sighed. She pointed at the machines. The whole building site could be seen now that all the walls of the toilet block had been knocked down. 'We shall use the rumble stick, the sludge cauldron and the great smashing ball!' She smiled. Her face glowed with the success she could see in her mind's eye.

William and Ambrose still stared at Edith. 'The *what?*' asked Ambrose. William blinked and looked at the floor.

Perhaps Edith will forget I'm here, if I'm really lucky, he hoped.

'Give me *strength* . . .' Edith sighed. 'Let me make this clear. We're going to use the builders' tools to crush the school – *forever!*' She threw back her head and cackled, shrieking like a banshee.

Edith cleared her throat and smoothed her hair. 'Right. Jump to it then!' She rubbed her hands and crossed her arms, settling down to watch. 'Go on – get on with it! You useless pair, I don't know why I bother . . .' she nagged.

'I wish you didn't!' murmured Ambrose. William looked at Ambrose with wide, frightened eyes. Ambrose shrugged and walked towards the pneumatic drill. 'Just follow my lead, son – and don't look so worried. We'll manage to throw a spanner in the works yet!' he winked.

Ambrose grabbed hold of the drill and felt around the handle. He frowned and pressed down hard. He put it down and walked round it. He looked at it as though he'd lost something. Then he picked it up again and shook it.

William caught on. He flicked a switch on the concrete mixer gently and nothing happened. He walked round the mixer, scratching his head and chewing a nail. He frowned and kicked the mixer bowl.

'Can't seem to get it to work, Edith . . .' sighed Ambrose, sadly. He winked at William behind Edith's back. 'These new-fangled machines . . . they didn't have things like this back in my day.' He scratched his head.

'The sludge cauldron won't work either . . . I don't know what to do, Edith . . .' William whined.

'For goodness' *sake*!' screeched Edith, leaping up and creating a cloud of dust. 'If you want something done . . .' She rushed towards the cement mixer. William hid behind Ambrose. 'Don't ask idiots to do it!' she shouted.

She pulled a lever and the cement mixer rumbled into action. '*See!*' she roared. 'I've made it work!' She pushed Ambrose and William out of the way. 'I'll do it all myself, if I have to!' she shrieked.

William tripped over some rubble and landed in the dust.

'Stop messing about, boy!' Edith shouted.

She pressed a button and the pneumatic drill made a terrible rattling noise. 'There! No problem! The sludge cauldron and the judder stick are working. Now *get on with it*!' Edith spat.

William reached out for the drill handle. As he grabbed it with one hand, he shook and jiggled. When he tried holding on with both hands he started to rattle up and down.

'I c-c-c-can't control it!' he wailed, bouncing across the playground as though he was on a demon pogo stick.

But Edith wasn't listening. She'd jumped into the cab of the wrecking ball, her eyes shining red. 'St Sebastian's, prepare to meet your doom!' she cackled.

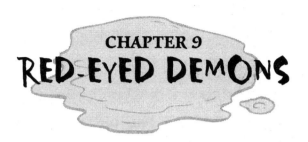

CHAPTER 9
RED-EYED DEMONS

'Those ridiculous builders!' exclaimed Mr Tick, reaching for his coat. 'Miss Keys! Cancel that police call. There's no need for alarm. I shall deal with this personally!' Mr Tick raised his chin and smiled down at his secretary.

'Oh, headmaster . . .' she sighed, watching as he swept from the room.

'Boys! I told you to get back to your classrooms! Do so *immediately*!' Mr Tick thundered, discovering James, Alexander and Lenny peering through the glass of the rear doors to the playground.

'But, Dad!' Alexander whinged. Mr Tick's nostrils flared.

He put his face so close to Alexander's that the boy could see his nose hair bristling.

'What . . . did . . . I . . . say . . . about calling me that childish name at school? Nine o'clock to three-twenty! It's not difficult! This is your last warning, boy . . .' Alexander stepped back. Mr Tick pulled himself up to his full height. 'GET BACK TO YOUR CLASSROOMS!' he shouted. Then another loud crash from outside sent him running out into the playground.

The boys ran to an upstairs window to get a better view of the action.

'I think we should go back to the classroom, guys – what if your dad comes back, Stick? You don't want to get in any more trouble . . .' whispered Lenny.

'I'm not sure that's actually possible,' Alexander sighed deeply.

81

Mr Tick dashed across the tarmac towards the site of the toilet block, his tie flapping over his shoulder.

'He can run quite fast, your dad . . .' said James, raising his eyebrows at Alexander.

Mr Tick was waving his fists at the builders. They took no notice.

'It's like a weird silent film, isn't it?' James said. 'Except for all the crashing and banging, of course!'

The headmaster tried to run in front of the machines, waving his arms to get attention. None of the builders seemed to see him.

'Look,' said James. 'There's a tall builder over there chasing a smaller one around. And isn't that a pneumatic drill he's riding?'

'Oh, no – what's my dad doing *now*?' Alexander cried. The headmaster had grabbed the youngest builder by the shoulders as he shook past on the drill. The boys watched in horror as the headmaster was carried across the playground, dragged behind it.

'We should go and help him. What if he gets hurt?' said Lenny.

'I don't think he'll put himself in any *real* danger,' sighed Alexander. Mr Tick let go of the drill and tumbled to the ground. 'Uh-oh, that's torn it. Now his posh suit's got all dirty . . .' muttered Alexander.

The headmaster stood up and brushed himself off. He glared at the builder working the cement mixer and marched across to talk to him. He tried to push the builder out of the way to get at the controls. The builder reached out with a meaty hand and held him off. Mr Tick's arms were waving and he was walking on the spot, trying to get closer to the machine.

'Poor Dad . . .' Alexander whispered.

Mr Tick jumped back from the cement mixer. A huge blob of porridgy cement plopped out of the mixer and covered his feet. Alexander winced. 'Not the Italian leather . . .' he groaned. The headmaster stared down at his feet with wide eyes. His head snapped up and he gritted his teeth. He launched himself at the third builder with a growl.

'Oh, no! Not the wrecking ball!' said James, watching the builder in the cab of the wrecking ball fight with the controls. 'It looks a bit like one of those things at the arcade that you get to pick up toys. Except it has a ball instead of a grabber . . .' he mused.

'So, it's actually nothing like one then,' snapped Alexander. 'Can we focus, please, James? That is still my *dad* out there!'

'Sorry, Stick – I keep forgetting,' James smiled.

The wrecking ball jerked and bounced for a moment, then the truck zoomed torwards Mr Tick.

'He'll be squished like a bug!' shouted Alexander, covering his eyes with his hands.

85

He peered through gaps in his fingers. 'I can't watch!' he groaned. The headmaster's mouth hung open as he saw the truck heading straight for him. '*Run*, Dad!' Alexander called.

As though he'd heard him, Mr Tick began to move. At first, he ran stiffly like a clockwork model, looking over his shoulder. As the truck roared behind him, picking up speed, so did Mr Tick. He sprinted hard across the playground, his arms and legs pumping up and down.

'Hey, that's pretty impressive for an old guy,' gasped James. Alexander shot him a look. 'Sorry, I forgot again,' James apologised.

With a roar like a frustrated animal, the machine screeched to a halt as Mr Tick thundered through the double doors of the school's back entrance.

'Look at the builder!' hissed James, pressing himself against the window.

In the cab of the wrecking ball, a builder was snorting like an angry bull. His face was bright red, and an unearthly purple glow completely surrounded him.

'He looks like some sort of alien from a film!' said James.

'Or a ghost . . .' said Alexander, turning to face him.

They all turned back to look at the builder. His eyes were glowing red.

'Is it just me —' began Lenny.

'Yes. Flames. In his eyes. Yup, I see them too,' Alexander shuddered.

A sudden bellow from the corridor beneath them made them all jump.

'Run to your classrooms! Take shelter under your desks!' It was Mr Tick, as he crashed through the fire doors and ran for cover. 'Hide anywhere! Just take cover!' his voice travelled as he ran.

'Quick! He's coming up the stairs!' James hissed at his friends.

Lenny stepped back into an alcove and hid behind a bookcase and James crouched behind a supplies cupboard, but Alexander just stood there rooted to the spot.

'Stick! Stick! Move it *now*!' shouted James. But it was no use. Alexander just stood goggling at the stairway.

James grabbed him by the arm, tugging him hard until he slumped down next to him behind the cupboard.

'It's OK – I think he's heading for his office,' whispered Lenny, peeping out from behind the bookcase.

The boys heard Mr Tick slam the door to his room and the sound of what must have been his desk being pushed across to block it. There was a swish as the blinds were pulled down, then everything went quiet.

The boys slid out from their hiding places.

'Do you think he's OK?' Alexander asked, flicking his thumb down towards the headmaster's study.

'Only one way to find out!' James whispered. 'Let's have a listen.'

They crept down the stairs. James bent and pressed his ear against the door.

'Well?' asked Alexander.

'I think you'd better listen yourself,' James said, stepping back to make room.

Alexander crouched down and pressed an ear to his dad's office door. 'Oh, dear . . .' he said, looking at the others. 'Erm . . . I can hear him kind of babbling. "Red eyes" . . . "demons" . . . "monsters" – that sort of thing – and a kind weird giggling.'

'I'd take that as a great big *not* OK then, Alexander . . .' said Lenny, patting his friend on the shoulder.

Alexander stood up and sighed. 'Well, at least he's safe in there – for now.'

CHAPTER 10
ARMED AND DANGEROUS

'Come on – let's go upstairs again and check the staffroom,' said James.

Whooping and laughing could be heard coming from above. A gang of year eights ran past kicking a school bag and Alexander went bright red at the thought of his dad hiding in his room.

The staffroom was quiet.

'Let's push the door and see if it opens. If it does, we can say you were looking for your dad,' suggested James.

Alexander walked towards the door slowly. He reached out a shaking hand. 'Blimey, Stick – it's not going to explode!' Lenny laughed.

Alexander smiled and tried to open the door. 'It's bolted shut.' The room looked dark through the frosted glass – the blinds must be drawn.

'OK – so that's the grown ups out of action then . . . it's up to us now!' said James, putting his arms around Alexander and Lenny's shoulders. They stepped to one side as some year tens pushed past, carrying piles of books.

'Well, I'm not staying if there are no teachers . . .' one of the girls said.

A group of year sevens ran past in a hail of paper balls. 'Cool – paper wars!' laughed Lenny. His face dropped as he saw Leandra coming along the corridor towards him. Stacey trailed behind her as usual.

'All right, titch?' she asked gruffly grabbing Lenny by the arm.

'Titch? I'd make two of you!' said Lenny, pulling his arm away. His cheeks flushed. 'I'm fine, Leandra. I don't need a nursemaid, you know.'

'Yeah . . . sure . . . whatever!' she cuffed his ear. 'Does anyone know what's going on? I mean, no one turned up to teach third period in any classes. There are gangs of kids running around everywhere and others are just grabbing their stuff and going home. Plus, there's loads of noise coming from the playground.'

Right on cue, there was a huge crash. Stacey jumped and hid behind Leandra.

'And what's with all these rumours about the builders?' She put out her hand and grabbed the jacket of a terrified year seven.

'Let me go! There are aliens outside! They're glowing funny colours and they've got red eyes!' he struggled. Leandra released the boy and he ran off.

'See?' she said. 'What's going on?'

'You'll never believe it . . .' Lenny sighed, and began to explain.

'Ghosts? You *have* to be kidding me!' Leandra scoffed. 'I thought the builders had been driven mad by Mr Tick!'

'And we're on our own,' said James. 'Mr Tick is . . . er . . .' He looked at Alexander.

'Basically, he's hiding,' shrugged Alexander.

'To be fair,' said Lenny, 'so are the rest of the teachers. They're holed up in the staffroom with the door locked.'

'So it's up to us,' said James.

'We're in,' said Leandra, fiercely.

'We need a plan though,' said Alexander, rubbing a hand over his chin.

'Well, we know the ghosts can be damaged, at least in builder form,' said James. 'That club

hammer smashed the first ghost's finger off.
We saw that in the toilets.'

'Yuck!' Stacey shuddered. 'I don't want to
hurt anybody.'

'Well, they aren't really *anybody*,' said
Alexander. 'They were *once* – but now they are
just a kind of residual energy . . . you know, left
behind when . . .'

'They're evil spirits! Like in "Zombie Dance!"'
laughed James.

'Not quite, James. Firstly, that's a computer
game. Secondly, zombies would be more
corporeal – you know, they'd actually have a
solid body . . . well, possibly a slightly liquid
body, with all that rotting . . .' Alexander
continued, self-importantly.

'OK, professor – whatever!' said James. 'Perhaps
that's not quite the thing to focus on right
now . . .?'

'Sorry . . .' Alexander muttered.

'I think what he means is, you can't actually *hurt* their bodies, because their bodies aren't real,' said Lenny. Stacey smiled so brightly he forgot what he was going to say next.

'Well, count me in then!' she said. Leandra patted her back.

'That's the spirit! Heh, heh, *spirit* – get it?' she laughed. Everyone groaned.

'But what can we do?' said James. 'We can't let the ghosts take over. St Sebastian's might be a bit of a dump, but it's *our* dump! The teachers aren't going to do anything about it . . . no offence, Stick . . . so we'll definitely need a plan of attack!'

'OK,' said Leandra. 'Why don't we split up and search the school for weapons? There are tools everywhere . . .'

'We can get loads from the science and technology labs – plenty of goodies there!' said Alexander.

96

'And the kitchen – loads of sharp things in there!' added Stacey.

'Right,' said James. 'It's a plan. We'll split up and collect what we can and meet back here in quarter of an hour.'

CHAPTER 11
A CUNNING PLAN

'She's finally gone completely mad!' shouted Ambrose. The noise was deafening. 'She's trying to squash everyone!'

Edith was roaring about the playground in the wrecking-ball cab, cackling to herself and swinging the ball at anyone who went past. Mrs Cooper, one of the dinner ladies, scuttled out of the canteen and ran wildly for the safety of the main building.

'Come back!' shrieked Edith, swinging the ball. 'Stop running about and stand still.' The dinner lady sobbed as she ran. She tripped on some rubble. 'I've got you now!' yelled Edith. Lynn scrabbled through the fire doors in to safety.

A group of year sevens was thundering towards the front gates. Edith shot after them. The cab rocked dangerously as she cornered the main building. She swung the ball at the boys and they dived through the school gates with shrieks and wails. The ball rushed through the air, sailing through the space where their heads had been.

'Stupid boys!' Edith screamed after them.

One small girl dropped her lunchbox and bent to pick it up as Edith took another wild swing with the ball. It came within centimetres of the girl's head, blowing her fringe back off her face. She flung herself through the gates with a sob.

William watched in horror as he continued to wrestle with the drill. He bounced up and down, catching flashes of what Edith was up to, holding tight to the drill handle until his fingers went white. He waved a hand over his head at Ambrose and the drill tipped sideways.

'Ambrose! Ambrose! Look over here! I need you!' he shouted. Ambrose didn't look up. 'This is so noisy – I can't get his attention . . .' William moaned.

'Ambrose!' he shouted, louder this time. The drill rattled like a train on bumpy tracks. 'Ambrose! I'm getting shaken apart!' he yelled. Tiny blobs of ectoplasm were tearing away from William's body. 'HELP ME!' he screeched.

But Ambrose was busy. He stuck a big, meaty finger into the cement. 'Looks like porridge . . .' he muttered. He scooped up a big lumpy dollop and licked it off his finger, rolling the cement round in his mouth to savour the full flavour of the gooey paste. He stuck out his tongue and looked at it. His eyes crossed and he curled his top lip. 'Delicious!' he exclaimed.

He looked up and saw William. 'What are you
doing, son?' he asked. William waved his arms.
'Hello to you, too! Enjoying yourself?' he smiled.
William waved again and jumped as a strip of
ectoplasm peeled off his leg. 'Steady, lad . . .'
Ambrose shouted.

He started to move towards William. 'Do you
need help, son?' William rolled his eyes – at last!

'I'm coming!' Ambrose called. 'Hang on, lad!' He coughed and spat a wodge of cement on to the floor. A leech tugged itself out of the centre of the pile and inched off, leaving a sticky, grey trail behind it.

By the time Ambrose reached him, William had managed to turn the drill down. He still rattled, but was no longer losing bits of body.

'You all right, son?' Ambrose asked.

'F-f-fine!' stuttered William. We need to —'

Crash, rattle, bang!

'Sorry, son? What was that? We need to what?'

'We can stop —' *Bang, rattle!*

Ambrose frowned. He stuck a finger in his ear and waggled it. He pulled it out and examined the mucky prize on his fingertip. Sucking his finger, he tried again. 'I can't hear you — speak up!'

William's words were lost again in a series of noises. He pointed at Edith. Then he drew a line across his neck with his finger.

'Kill Edith? Sorry, son, you're a bit late for that. Can see the attraction though . . .' he chuckled.

William shook his head and scowled. He pointed at Edith again.

'Yup, Edith – got it . . .' encouraged Ambrose. William held up a hand like a traffic policeman.

'I don't think waving at Edith will help . . .' Ambrose said.

William shook his head again and slumped over the drill. He tried one more time. He pointed at Edith. They watched her chase Mr Wharpley across the playground. He was throwing bottles of disinfectant at the cab as he ran.

'He's game!' laughed Ambrose. Mr Wharpley screamed and swore as Edith caught up with him. 'I don't think that'll stop her . . . Stop her!' The penny dropped. 'You want us to *stop* her!'

'Too right!' Mr Wharpley bellowed, as he dived into the boiler house just in the nick of time.

William gave Ambrose a thumbs-up sign.
'But how?' asked the older ghost.

William pointed at the cement mixer and
made a spinning motion with his finger.

'The sludge cauldron? Not very tasty, I'm afraid. Don't think we have time for a snack anyway, if we're going to stop Edith . . .' said Ambrose. 'Why are you screaming, William? Something the matter?' He leant in closer to his young friend.

The boy's eyes were screwed up with the effort of trying to make Ambrose understand. He took a deep breath and tried again. He made a pouring movement with his hand and pointed at the wrecking-ball cab.

'You want to throw the sludge at Edith? Don't we all . . .' Ambrose sighed. He leant in closer and cupped his hand behind his ear.

William flinched as he saw things crawling about in the hole, but came closer and shouted into it.

'Well, I never knew the sludge would do that!' Ambrose laughed. 'Good thing you watched those other builders make that new sewer outlet a while back!' Then he frowned and stuck out his tongue. He scraped his filthy fingernails across it and shook his hand hard. Muck slid off his fingers and flew through the air.

A blob hit William on the corner of his mouth. He retched, but managed a watery smile. At last, they had a plan.

CHAPTER 12
THE BUBONIC BATTLE

'Right – this is it, everyone. I don't have to tell you, it's dangerous out there,' said James. The friends were crouching in a group, watching the builders through a window.

The wrecking ball swung past, aimed at Mr Wharpley, who'd just poked his head out of the boiler-house door.

'Wow! What a dive! Old Mr Wharpley could be goalie for Grimesford United with skills like that!' Leandra laughed. Lenny smiled at his sister.

'OK – we're all armed. Does everyone know what to do?' James asked, looking around at the circle.

Alexander held up a bag of maggots. 'I found these fly larvae by the school bins.' The bag seethed with what looked like fat, white macaroni – with heads. Stacey squealed and hid her face in her scarf.

'They look like maggots to me . . . ' said James. He rattled a hot-glue gun. 'Well, the teachers are always saying these things are dangerous – so here's my chance to prove it!' he laughed.

Stacey peeped out of her hiding place. 'I've got this bottle of perfume I've been wanting to get rid of, but my nan gave it to me, so I didn't want to just chuck it out. I left it in my locker at school. It's good for getting marks off things . . .' She trailed off, looking down at the floor. Leandra glanced at her friend.

'What? Perfume? How's that a weapon, Stacey?'

'Well, sniff it,' Stacey said, taking the lid off the sparkly pink bottle. Leandra leant in for a sniff and her head shot backwards, her eyes screwing up with disgust.

'Phwoah! It's enough to make you throw up! Point taken, Stacey. One squirt in the face with that and they'll be completely knocked out!' Stacey smiled. 'I've got this loudhailer, so I can coordinate things – I took it from the PE cupboard.'

'Boss people about, you mean . . .' grumbled Lenny. Leandra ignored him.

'*And* I've got a lino cutter from the art room,' she added, waving the tool in the air.

'Well, I've got this,' said Lenny, holding a javelin like a staff.

'Ooh! You'll look like a gladiator!' Stacey giggled. Lenny's face went crimson.

'Well – we're ready. Time to huddle up before we go . . .' said James.

'Cuddle up? I don't think so . . .' said Alexander, looking horrified.

'No, swotboy!' James laughed, scrubbing Alexander's hair with his knuckles. 'A *huddle* – like in rugby before you all go in to action!'

'Oh . . .' It was Alexander's turn to go red.

The team bunched together and patted each other's backs. They made their fists into a ring at the centre of the circle and then threw their hands up in the air.

'For St Sebastian's!' yelled Leandra, and they charged down the stairs, out of the fire doors and into battle.

Ambrose turned to see where the noise was coming from. A gang of children was running towards him. They were waving things in the air. 'William . . . these kids don't look very friendly . . .' he called.

William spun round to see Lenny running straight at him with a long, pointed stick. He smiled to see the kids taking charge – and the smile slid off his face as he realised that he was the enemy, too!

He leapt off the drill, leaving it spinning in a noisy circle on the ground, and started to run.

Ambrose hid behind the cement mixer. A girl holding a sparkly pink bottle crept up behind him. William pointed to her and Ambrose spun round.

'Arrgh!' screamed Ambrose. 'A witch with a bottle of poison!'

'Eeeek!' shrieked Stacey. 'A horrid fat man with rotten teeth!'

Ambrose frowned. 'Rotten teeth? I'll have you know not many people my age have stumps as fine as these!'

Stacey scowled. 'Witch? Do I *look* like I have a warty nose?'

Edith's screeches of rage cut through their argument. She was driving straight towards William's friends!

111

'Quick, Ambrose!' shouted William. 'Help me tip this over!' He was struggling with the cement mixer, pushing it with his shoulder. The mixer wobbled, but didn't fall. 'It's too heavy!' he cried.

'Our plan! Of *course*!' yelled Ambrose. He flashed his teeth at Stacey and grabbed the cement mixer as she shuddered. He heaved his shoulder under the mixer bowl. 'Come on, sludge cauldron – *shift*!' he grunted.

Lenny whacked the javelin against the window of the wrecking-ball cab. The builder inside gnashed his teeth and flecks of slimy yellow spittle sprayed on the windscreen.

Stacey sprayed puffs of perfume at Ambrose. He swatted at her as though she were an annoying fly. 'Get away, witch! Can't you see I'm busy with this here sludge cauldron?' he growled. Stacey battled on.

Leandra was slashing at the tyres of the cab with the lino cutter. The wrecking ball swung dangerously close to her head. 'Keep it up, troops!' she yelled through the loudhailer.

Alexander threw a handful of maggots into Ambrose's face. 'Not sure it's time for snacks, lad – but I appreciate the effort!' he grunted, picking a clump of them off his chin and popping it into his mouth with a crunch.

Alexander's face went pale and he felt bile rise into his throat. He spat on the floor.

'You all right?' called Stacey.

'Yeah . . . but I was just a bit sick in my mouth
. . .' he shuddered.

James was squirting molten glue at any ghost
who came within range. William was getting
tangled in a web of glue strands as he wrestled
with the mixer.

The wrecking ball swung at Lenny, knocking
the javelin out of his hand. 'Ouch! My arm!'
he yelled.

'If we don't do something soon, Edith will really hurt someone!' William fretted.

With a heave, he and Ambrose finally managed to topple the mixer. A volcano of cement erupted from the bowl. It raced across the tarmac in a wave of grey – right in the path of the wrecking-ball cab.

Edith's eyes widened as she saw the cement flowing towards her. Her head whipped from side to side, looking for an escape route. She was trapped. The huge wheels turned slowly, gummed up with sticky cement.

Edith glared at William, her red eyes glowing and flashing. 'You stupid boy! I'll have you exorcised for this!' she hissed. William started to shiver.

'*Exorcised?* Why would she want you *exercised?*' laughed Ambrose, jabbing William with his elbow. William tried to smile. 'I would have thought we'd had enough of that lately!'

115

116

Edith yanked the lever backwards and forwards, trying to release the wheels. She was stuck. She shrieked, and everyone covered their ears.

CHAPTER 13
REST IN PIECES

Preventing themselves from going deaf meant the gang had to put down their weapons.

'What a choice!' shouted Leandra. 'Listening to this racket or letting those stupid bubonic ghosts win!'

James could see right into the screaming builder's mouth. *That gives me an idea . . .* he thought, and he shot a stream of melted glue into the air.

It slid straight down Edith's throat. She gulped, then swallowed – and the noise ceased.

'Thank goodness!' shouted Alexander. The gang cheered James.

The builder's eyes bulged. A thick vein, like a pale worm, throbbed on his forehead. He clawed at his throat.

Lenny cheered, then saw the cab start to jerk. 'It's out of control – and it's heading straight for the school!' he yelled, pointing at the wrecking-ball machine.

James leapt on to it, heaving himself into the cab. He pulled at the bubonic builder inside, trying to get hold of the lever. The man shrieked in his face and flailed a meaty hand at him. He was so close he caught a waft of foul breath. It was like sewer water . . . or a dead, rotting rat . . . James coughed.

He tugged at the fat hand, trying to pull the fingers off the lever one by one. The builder poked at James's eye with a stubby finger, but missed and picked his nose violently instead.

119

James fell back against the window of the cab.

'James!' Alexander shouted. He was flinging a hail of maggots at William, who was making choking noises. Alexander dropped the bag and ran towards the truck.

Stacey was squirting a ton of perfume at Ambrose who was coughing and spluttering. She threw down the empty bottle and ran towards James.

The bottle smashed against Ambrose's boots and a cloud of sugary scent rose up around him. '*Yaargh! It's horrible!*' be bellowed, covering his face.

James rubbed his head as he sat up. He gritted his teeth and yanked on the bubonic builder's arm, wedging his feet against the side of the truck as he pulled. He felt a tearing sensation. It was like pulling the leg off a roast chicken for Sunday lunch.

The man's arm had come away from the lever, but it had also come away from his body. Green

121

goo flooded out of the hole. Strings of slime, like raw egg white, slid through James's fingers. He shivered and dropped the arm. As it shrivelled, the fingers curled into a claw and grabbed James's leg.

He kicked the arm and it flew out of the cab, slapping Lenny in the face as he ran to help. A trail of green slime gushed from it, covering his friend with a slimy layer of gum.

'*Erk! Blah!*' Lenny shrieked, wiping his eyes. A thin layer of the stuff still covered his mouth. He opened his lips and tasted the goo with the tip of his tongue. He shrieked, blowing a bubble with the slime that left his mouth and sailed into the air. It popped on Stacey's cheek.

'Yuck! Get it off!' she squealed.

James pushed at the builder's body, which was slumped against him. It toppled sideways and fell from the cab. There was a sound like a box of eggs hitting the floor.

'You've done it!' Alexander cheered. 'It appears to be deceased – again.' He bent over the corpse. Slime still oozed from the hole where the arm had been. The head lolled to one side and the face was starting to shrivel.

'Wow, it looks like something from *The Mummy*!' shouted Lenny. 'Come on, Stick, we don't need to watch this.' He put his arm round Alexander's shoulder and they turned to look at James, who was waving his hands at them both.

'Are you OK?' Lenny shouted.

'What? We can't hear you – hang on,' said Alexander, stepping closer to the truck. 'Do you want us to do something?' Then he went stiff as he saw what James was doing. His friend was pulling the lever and swinging the ball straight at him!

He grabbed Lenny and they rolled across the tarmac. The ball swung through the space where Alexander had been – straight into the dead builder's head!

123

There was a horrible snapping sound, like
a dry stick being trodden on. The man looked
shocked for a moment, then his head rolled
off his shoulders and landed with a squelch on
the ground.

James stumbled down from the cab. Leandra
grabbed him. 'You did it . . .' she whispered.

'We *all* did,' he smiled. The friends watched
as the builder started to shrivel. 'Hey, look!

It's happening to the other two as well!'
Stacey shouted.

Wisps of green gas floated into the air. A
sparrow flew through one and dived suddenly
into a bush, screeching.

The builder's remaining hand felt about on the
floor for the head, moving like a huge, ugly spider.
His face began to melt. His cheeks caved in,
leaving dark hollows. His nose sank, then deflated
like an old balloon. His bloodshot eyes were the
last thing to go. They stared angrily at James for
a moment and, with a wet 'pop', they were gone.
A sticky puddle lay sinking into the tarmac.

'Gross!' cried Stacey, wafting her hand in front
of her face.

'I thought *you'd* been possessed, when you
swung that wrecking ball at me!' Alexander
laughed, putting his arm round James's shoulder.

'Sorry, Stick – but when I saw that builder
rear up, slashing the air with his arm and trying

to grab you, I didn't know what else to do!' smiled James.

'Well,' said Alexander, 'I'm glad you didn't lose your head – and that's more than can be said for *some* people . . .!' There was a chorus of groans.

The fire doors to the back entrance slammed. Mr Tick came marching towards the gang. He grabbed the loudhailer from Leandra and held it to his mouth. There was an ear-splitting whine.

'Feedback!' winced Lenny.

'It would all be bad, if it was about Mr Tick!' James laughed. Alexander stuck his tongue out at James and pushed him in the shoulder.

'Right, everyone, listen up!' the headmaster boomed importantly. 'I have made sure everything is quite safe now. Those so-called builders have left the premises, so there is absolutely nothing to fear.'

'Listen to him – taking charge again as soon as we're out of danger!' Lenny grumbled. 'Not a word of thanks, of course . . .'

'You may all take the afternoon as home study leave, while Mr Wharpley clears up this rather unfortunate mess,' he continued.

The caretaker stuck his head out of the boiler house. 'Oh, yes, it would be me . . . single-handed, of course. Can't have anyone else getting their hands dirty, oh, no . . .' he grumbled, as he climbed out into the light.

'Run along now, everybody!' said Mr Tick, as the gang stared at him. He pulled Alexander to one side. 'Alexander, tell your mother I shall be late. I'm off to the golf . . . ahem, county hall to talk to the authorities about this mess. I may be some time . . .' He hurried towards his office.

'The cheek! Sorry, Stick – I know he's your dad, but . . .' frowned James.

Lenny punched them both playfully on the shoulder. 'Look at it this way, the ghosts have gone and we've got the afternoon off! I think it's time for a game of football. You in?' he said to the girls.

'Too right!' Leandra said.

They clattered out of the gates, leaving an empty playground. Empty, that is, apart from a rotting lump that had once been an arm and the echo of Edith Codd's angry shriek, 'I'm not finished with you yet, St Sebastian's . . .'

SURNAME: Codd

FIRST NAME: Edith

AGE: 602

HEIGHT: 1.65 metres

EYES: Red and glowing

HAIR: Ginger, wiry and full of dandruff

FACT FILE

LIKES: Shouting and screaming (especially at the other plague-pit ghosts), finding new and ingenious ways to get rid of St Sebastian's and everyone in it

DISLIKES: Noisy kids stopping her from resting in peace and getting her 'beauty' sleep

SPECIAL SKILL: Getting her own way

INTERESTING FACT: When she was alive, Edith was married. Her long-suffering husband survived the Black Death whereas she did not, much to the relief of his eardrums

For more facts on Edith Codd, go to **www.too-ghoul.com**

How to Keep Your Toilet GIRL FREE*

By Alexander Tick, year seven

*Because you just CAN'T GO when girls are around!

- Stick a fake spider to the loo-roll holder. Eugh!

- Drop a stink bomb down one of the toilets. The waft will warn them off!

- Pour some green food colouring into the water to create a haunted toilet effect

- Get some jelly worms and dangle them out of the taps

- Remove all the mirrors, so girls won't be able to do their hair!

- Hide a CD player in the room that blasts out ghoulish screams and gurgles

- If all else fails, there's only one option . . . wee on the seat!**

** Don't try this at home. Mums have been known to make you clear it up afterwards!

How to Spot a Haunted Builder

A cut-out 'n' keep guide, by James Simpson

Glowing, red eyes

Uses tools to attack people, not fix stuff

Pasty, peeling skin

Eats cement, not biscuits

Immune to pain

Missing fingers and/or arms

Smells of rotting flesh

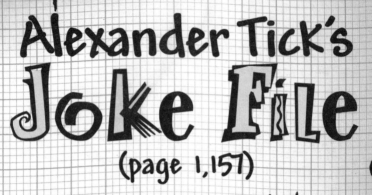

Alexander Tick's Joke File

(page 1,157)

Q Why don't skeletons fight each other?

A They don't have the guts!

Q Why did the pupil eat his homework?

A The teacher said it was a piece of cake!

Knock Knock

Who's there?

Carrie...

Carrie who?

Carrie on with what you were doing. I got the wrong house.

NOTE TO SELF: input these into jokes database at earliest convenience

Q Who did Frankenstein take to the cinema?

A His ghoul-friend!

Q What starts in a P, ends in an E and has a million letters in it?

A The post office!

Q Why should you take a pencil to bed?

A To draw the curtains!

Q Why do birds fly south?

A Cos it's too far to walk!

Q What do little cannibals play?

A Swallow the leader!

Q Why is Dracula so unpopular?

A Cos he's a pain in the neck!

Q What should you do if you see an elephant in your car?

A Buy a new car!

To see some of Alexander's joke database, visit www.too-ghoul.com

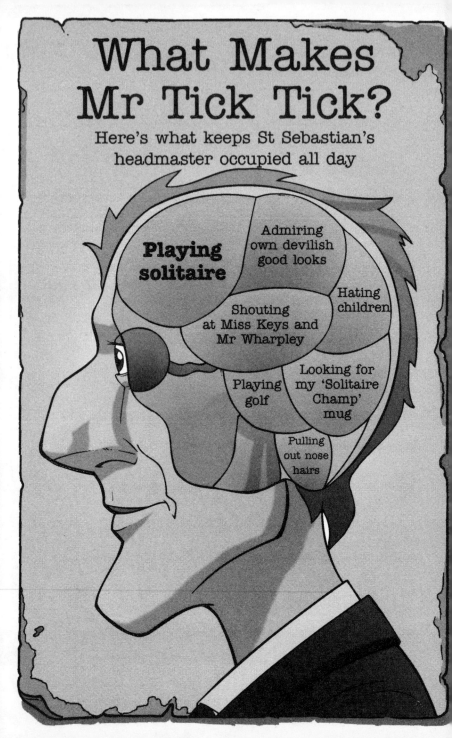

Can't wait for the next book in the series?
Here's a sneak preview of

SILENT BUT DEADLY

available now from all good bookshops,
or **www.too-ghoul.com**

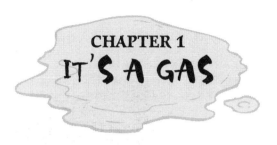

CHAPTER 1
IT'S A GAS

'Time for a terrific teacher's tinkle!' sang
Mr Watts to himself as he unzipped his trousers.
School would be starting in a little under fifteen
minutes' time and a pre-pupil pee was part of his
regular morning routine. It was a chance to run
through the day's schedule without interruptions.

'Double science with year seven to begin with,'
he said aloud, his voice echoing around the
empty staff toilets. 'Followed by break and a cup
of hot tea: two sugars, a splash of milk and a
bourbon biscuit.' Mr Watts was nothing if not

thorough. Science and precise measurements were his life.

As he continued with the timetable ahead, he failed to notice a faint hissing sound that came from one of the cubicles behind him.

Slowly, a cloud of dirty, green gas rose above the cubicle door and turned, seeming to look around the room. It spotted Mr Watts – now busy listing his lunch menu – and floated silently towards him.

'Four potatoes, microwaved for four point five minutes and smothered with approximately four point five milligrams of butter, two thousand, three hundred grains of salt and a light sprinkling of pepper . . .'

The cloud hovered just centimetres behind Mr Watts's head as he paused to zip up his flies. Moving towards the sink, he turned his scientific mind towards his choice of lunchtime meat.

'Roast beef, three slices, each two point five millimetres thick . . .' he began, as he strolled across the bathroom to the soap dispenser. The green cloud kept pace, just out of Mr Watts's vision as he spun the hot tap, pumped liquid soap on to his palms and began to wash.

The cloud braced itself, ready to pounce as soon as Mr Watts had finished rinsing his hands. Ready to overwhelm him – any minute now. Aaaaaany minute . . . now. What was taking this idiot so long? He was only washing his hands, not preparing for surgery!

The cloud sighed and took a moment to glance around the room. Catching sight of itself in the mirror, it floated over and examined what it saw.

Hmmm. A big, floating cloud, thought the big, floating cloud. *Not exactly the scariest shape ever. How terrifying would the science teacher find that? If he ever finished washing his hands and turned around, that was. Plus, cloud shapes were so last year. Definitely time for a change.*

Concentrating hard, the cloud began to rearrange its atoms, searching its limited memory banks for a form that would scare an obsessively clean science teacher. New shape achieved, the cloud turned once again to the mirror to study the horrifying creature it had now become.

A chicken. The cloud had morphed into a chicken.

What was it going to do as a chicken? Peck Mr Watts's calculator to pieces? Shaking its beak, the cloud tried again. Molecules exploded and reformed as the green gas changed shape once more. Ah, this felt better – arms, legs, a weapon in one hand! Let's take a look.

A court jester. A jolly court jester, complete with a stick of jingly bells. The cloud sighed again. Although it was an improvement on the chicken, there must be something scarier it could transform itself into. Perhaps if it searched a mind other than its own . . .

Relaxing, the cloud let its mind drift outside the staff toilets and in to the school beyond. If it could tap in to the consciousness of one or more of the pupils, it could scan their thoughts and take the shape of something that frightened them. Aha! There was a group of year-eight girls. Now to discover their darkest fears . . .

'Three carrots, pre-sliced, swimming in lukewarm water,' continued Mr Watts, still unaware of the mysterious green shape that hovered behind him.

The cloud's shape changed quickly as it leapt unnoticed from mind to mind, seeking out the nightmare visions lurking deep inside the girls' brains.

'One slice of bread with a thin smear of margarine . . .'

A vampire. A swamp monster. A fountain pen. *A fountain pen?* Who's scared of a fountain pen? Ah – here's something. Oh, yes, this one's good. This one's *very* good.

The cloud changed shape for a final time and smiled as Mr Watts dried his hands on a paper towel, whistling merrily.

'And that's lunch sorted!' Tossing the paper towel into the bin, Mr Watts leant in to the mirror to check his thin, chinstrap beard. As he ran his fingers lovingly over the wiry hair, he became aware of a figure standing at the next mirror along.

'Morning, Bob,' Mr Watts grinned at Mr Hall, the history teacher, while checking his nostrils for bogeys. 'How's the industrial revolution treating you?' The figure growled wetly and the smile on Mr Watts's face died as he realised that the person standing beside him wasn't St Sebastian's history teacher after all.

The zombie's arm shot forwards and a powerful, green hand grabbed Mr Watts by the throat. The science teacher stared in horror at the creature that was now lifting him a metre off the ground. Flakes of olive skin peeled away from the zombie's face and piercing red eyes stared down at him.

Mr Watts tried to speak, to plead for his life, but the zombie's grip on his throat was too tight and he could only manage a weak gargling sound. The zombie pulled the teacher forwards, until its nose was touching his. Its vile breath made Mr Watts's eyes water.

'Gggggurrh!' groaned the teacher, struggling to concentrate as blackness came ever closer.

I have to escape, he thought as a wave of unconsciousness began to sweep over him. *I must find a way to beat this ogre. But I know nothing about fighting monsters — I only know science. Perhaps I could use science . . .*

Biology? No — the creature's certainly not human, so I can't use biology against it. Chemistry? What is the monster made of? I don't know, so chemistry's no use. That just leaves physics. Physics!

As his last strands of consciousness began to slip away, Mr Watts swung his leg out at just the right velocity and felt, with satisfaction, his foot connect hard with the contents of the zombie's trousers.

The creature staggered backwards briefly before steadying itself and grabbing the teacher's tie. Swinging him round, the zombie sent him crashing to the floor.

Breathing hard, Mr Watts scrambled to his feet, massaging the bruises that were beginning to appear around his neck. He dashed for the door.

He only managed to turn the handle and open the door a crack before the zombie grabbed his ankle and dragged him back across the slippery floor of the toilets.

'No! Please!' screamed Mr Watts, as the monster rose above him, yellowing teeth bared. Green saliva dripped from a thick, green tongue.

The science teacher screwed his eyes shut as the zombie roared and pounced upon its prey.